Draw [face h]

D1549230

← face h[ere]

This book belongs

to. . . . .

For Momo

FIRST PUBLISHED 2003 BY WALKER BOOKS LTD
87 VAUXHALL WALK LONDON SE11 5HJ

THIS EDITION PUBLISHED 2004

10 9 8 7 6 5 4 3 2 1

© 2003, 2004 Bruce Ingman

The right of Bruce Ingman to be identified as author/illustrator
of this work has been asserted by him in accordance with the
Copyright, Designs and Patents Act 1988

THIS BOOK HAS BEEN TYPESET IN FUTURA BOOK

PRINTED IN CHINA

ALL RIGHTS RESERVED

British Library Cataloguing in Publication Data:
a catalogue record for this book is available from the British Library

ISBN 1-84428-456-5

TERMS AND CONDITIONS FOR READING THIS BOOK!

1. When you get to the end, say "Again, please".
2. Put book under the bed or somewhere safe.
3. No sticky fingers or ripping pages.
4. Lots of giggling.
5. Say please.
6. Look smart.
7. Say thank you!

Amelia
David
Daniel

Hannah
Jane

Boston
← 5521 km

Liz
Patrick

Sydney
↓ a long way

Photographs:

Toy Story (p 22) – Walt Disney Co.

King Kong (p 22) – RKO courtesy of The Kobal Collection

Star Wars (p 23) – Lucasfilm Ltd courtesy of The Kobal Collection

Thanks to Jessica Ingman, Cait Robertson and Ellie Robertson

My mum used to say, Danny,

Tidy up!

Tuck your shirt in!

OUTSIDE

NOW!

And take that **THING** with you.

I found all sorts ▬ of things...

Then one day ...

The finder of this charter is the new owner and ruler of this land.
By law.

I didn't waste any time ...

to be some **changes** around **here!**

I appointed my
TOP GANG.

I gave them identity cards and the secret password to get them entry to Top Gang HQ for secret meetings.

I set about ruling

my land.

List of Changes

1. Stay up late

2. Chips with everything

3. Treats all the time

4. Every Wednesday teachers to wear funny hats

5. Wild parties every week

6. Wear what you like

7. Make your mum + dad wait outside in the car while you visit the toyshop for hours & hours

8. Friends around every day

9. No dentists! No hairdressers!

10. ~~No~~ Pets in school

11. Mum + Dad in bed by 8 o'clock

IT'S OFFICIAL!

School

was so much more fun.

straight to my room.

My new rules were very popular.

But sometimes I had to put my

foot down...

Monday

Judge cabbage competition.

Tuesday

Open garden fête.

Wednesday

Launch ship.

Thursday

Judge beauty contest.

Friday

Open toothbrush factory.

Saturday

Attend opera concert.

Sunday

Open another garden fête.

Monday

Then one day an unexpected visitor from

CENTRAL OFFICE

came looking for me. There was more to being in charge than I thought.

I held a meeting →

a new job.

Any biscuits?

Minister of Counting

Minister of Spelling

Minister of More Boring Things

Minister of Boring Things

with all the ministers →

← and gave each one

Minister of Being Polite

Minister of Shaking Hands

Minister of Transport

Minister of Rainy Days

Minister of Tidying Up

But I kept the best one for myself:

S PROUDLY

MINISTER OF **FUN!**

Start again!